THE
MATCH

RUSSELL AYTO

BLOOMSBURY PUBLISHING
LONDON · OXFORD · NEW YORK · NEW DELHI · SYDNEY

The man.
His dog.

Work. Home.
Work. Home.
Work. Home.
Work. Home.
Work. Home.
Work. Home.

The MATCH.

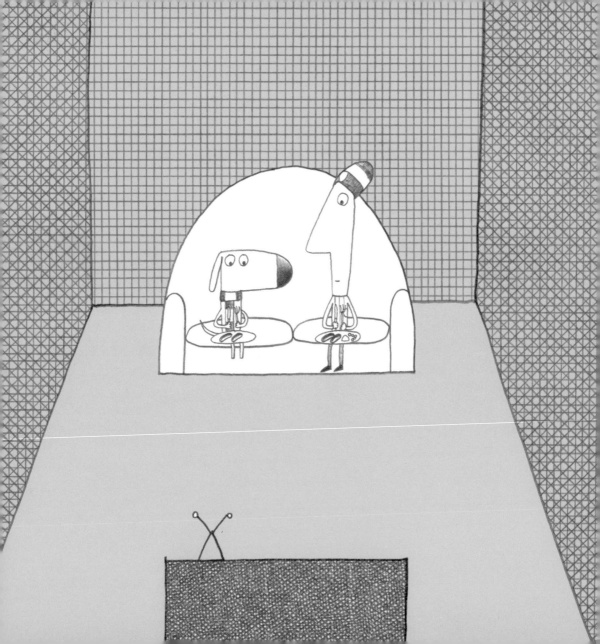

Clock. Ticking . . .

Ball. Kicking.
Whistle. Blowing.
Penalty. Missing.
Shirt. Pulling.
Red. Card.
Own. Goal.

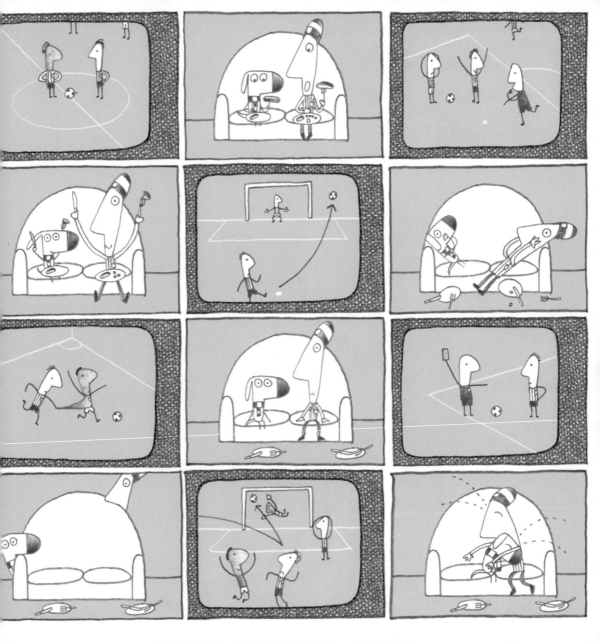

The DEFEAT.

Work. Home.
Work. Home.
Work. Home.
Work. Home.
Work. Home.
Work. Home.

The MATCH.

And the same old DEFEAT.

Work.
(The secret.)
Home.

The MATCH.

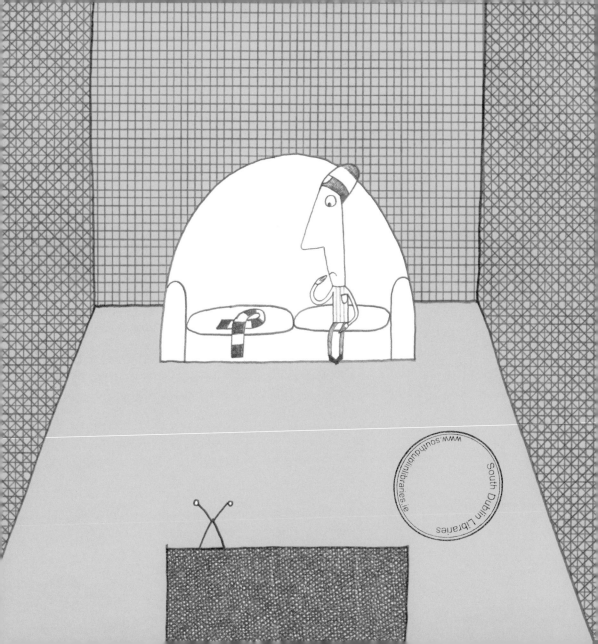

Clock. Ticking . . .

Ball. Kicking.
Fast. Passing.
Sharp. Shooting.
Tackle. Crunching.
Player. Injured.
Carried. Off . . .

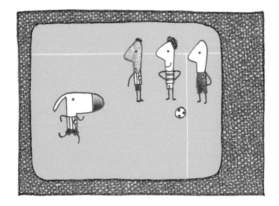

The "WHAT? I DON'T BELIEVE IT!" substitute.

And the . . .

"OH, WHAT A GOOAAALLLL!"

The dinner in the air.

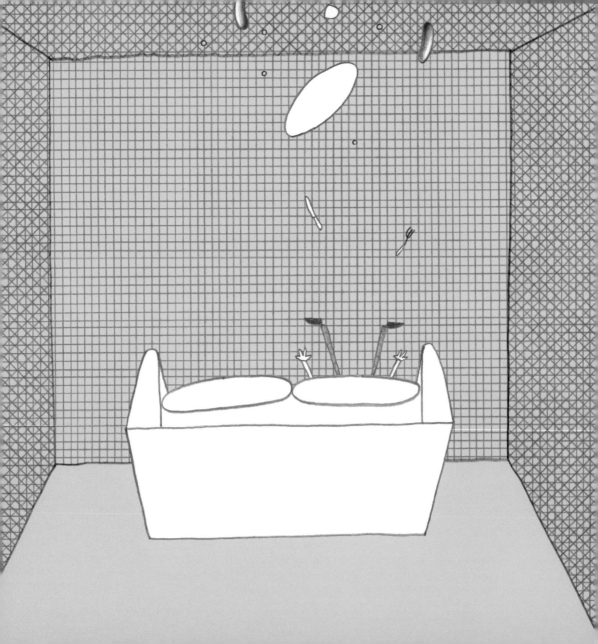

And . . .

The VICTORY!

The man.
His dog.
And the cup.

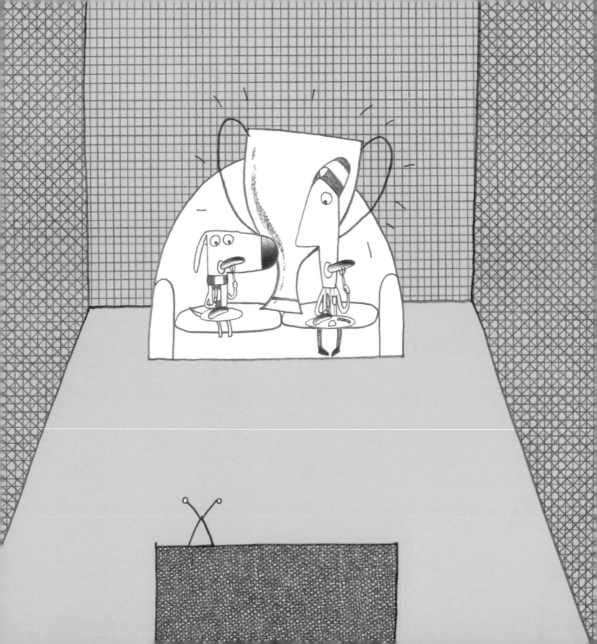

For the Terry Jones and the Michael Palin

BLOOMSBURY PUBLISHING
Bloomsbury Publishing Plc
50 Bedford Square, London, WC1B 3DP, UK

BLOOMSBURY, BLOOMSBURY PUBLISHING and the Diana logo are trademarks of Bloomsbury Publishing Plc

First published in Great Britain 2018 by Bloomsbury Publishing Plc

Text and illustrations © Russell Ayto, 2018

Russell Ayto has asserted his right under the Copyright, Designs and Patents Act, 1988,
to be identified as Author/Illustrator of this work

A catalogue record for this book is available from the British Library

ISBN: HB: 978-1-4088-9345-6

2 4 6 8 10 9 7 5 3 1

Printed and bound in China by Leo Paper Products, Heshan, Guangdong

Bloomsbury Publishing Plc makes every effort to ensure that the papers used in the manufacture
of our books are natural, recyclable products made from wood grown in well-managed forests.
Our manufacturing processes conform to the environmental regulations of the country of origin.

To find out more about our authors and books visit www.bloomsbury.com and sign up for our newsletters